BIG SARAH'S
LITTLE BOOTS

To Cheryl,
who always got my little boots
PB

For Sandy and Linda,
my big and little sisters
BC

Kids Can Press Ltd. gratefully acknowledges the assistance of the Canada Council and the Ontario Arts Council in the production of this book.

Canadian Cataloguing in Publication Data

Bourgeois, Paulette.
  Big Sarah's little boots

ISBN 0-921103-11-5 (bound)
ISBN 0-921103-70-0 (pbk.)

I. Clark, Brenda. II. Title.

PS8553.087B53 1987   jC813'.54   C87-093496-1
PZ7.B67Bi 1987

Text Copyright © 1987 by Paulette Bourgeois
Illustrations Copyright © 1987 by Brenda Clark

Kids Can Press Ltd.,
585½ Bloor Street West,
Toronto, Ontario, Canada, M6G 1K5.

Printed by Everbest Printing Co., Ltd., Hong Kong

PA 89 0 9 8 7 6 5 4

BIG SARAH'S
LITTLE BOOTS

WRITTEN BY
Paulette Bourgeois
ILLUSTRATED BY
Brenda Clark

Kids Can Press Ltd.
Toronto

Sarah loved her boots. They were as shiny as a wet slicker and as yellow as a bathtub duck. When Sarah jumped into puddles her boots went *SQUISH* and the water went *KERSPLAT!*

One day, Sarah tried to put on her boots. She pulled them and she tugged them. She scrunched her toes into tight little balls. She pushed her heels with all her might. But Sarah's boots did not fit Sarah's feet.

She took off her socks. But even bare, Sarah's feet did not fit into Sarah's boots.

"Oh, no!" cried Sarah. "My boots have shrunk."

Sarah tried to make her boots bigger. She stretched the bottoms and she stretched the tops.

She stretched until she could stretch no more.
But nothing happened.

Then she called her little brother Matthew. They tied one end of the boots to Matthew's horse and the other end to Sarah's bike.

They pulled until the ropes got tight.
But nothing happened.

Sarah gave the boots to the dog. He growled and tugged and she growled and tugged.

But nothing happened.

Sarah tried to blow them up like a balloon. She took a big breath and puffed her cheeks and blew. But nothing happened.

She filled her boots with a truckload of rocks. The boots got heavy, they didn't get bigger.

Sarah planted her boots in the garden where the sun was warm and bright. She watered them and she waited. But the boots did not grow.

Sarah was very sad. Her boots did not fit her feet. Her feet did not fit her boots. Sarah loved her boots.

"Mom," said Sarah, "my boots have shrunk."

"I wonder," said Sarah's mother. "Maybe you grew."

"No," said Sarah. "My boots have shrunk."

"Well, let's see," said Mother. Sarah was measured. "Your boots didn't shrink. You grew all over!" said Sarah's mother. "You need new boots."

"I don't want new boots," said Sarah.

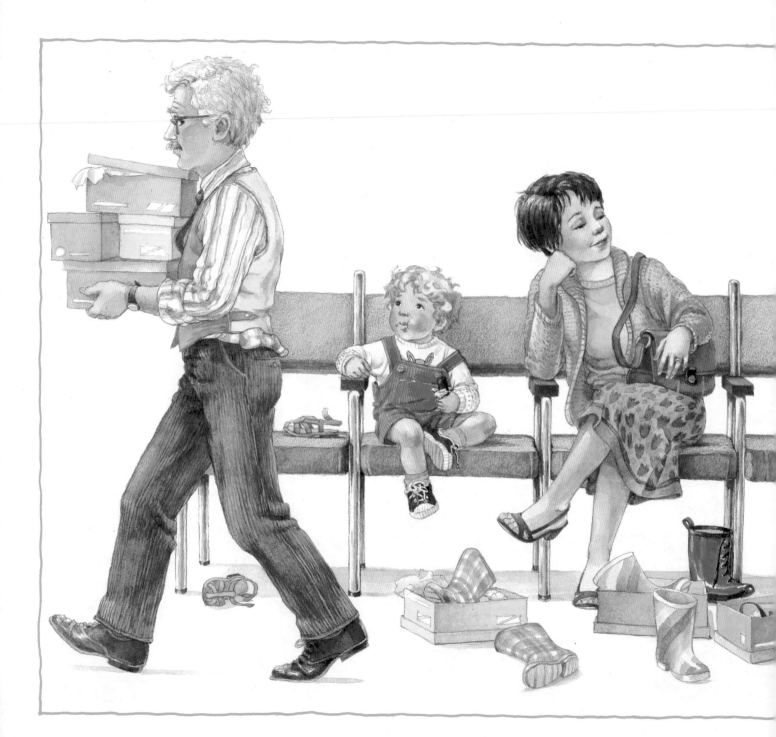

Sarah and her mother went to the store anyway. There were lots of boots - rainbow boots, red boots, purple boots, plaid boots, buckled boots and zippered boots.

The salesman showed Sarah yellow boots with a fire engine red stripe around the toes and a fire engine red stripe around the tops.

"These are lovely," said the salesman.
"I don't want new boots," said Sarah.

They bought the shiny yellow boots
with the fire engine red stripes.

The next time it rained, Sarah put on her new boots. They weren't as shiny or as yellow as her old boots. When Sarah jumped into puddles the water went *splash*, but that was all.

After a while, Sarah's mother asked if Matthew could wear the old boots.

Matthew looked so excited that Sarah said, "All right."

When Matthew put on the old boots he said, "These are so shiny. They're as yellow as my bathtub duck."

When Matthew jumped into a puddle the boots went
SQUISH and the water went *KERSPLAT!*

"I hope they don't shrink," said Matthew.

"Don't be silly," said Sarah. "Boots don't shrink, feet grow."

Matthew and Sarah went splashing in the puddles.
Suddenly, it didn't matter that Sarah's new boots went
splash and the old boots went *SQUISH*!

Sarah had grown so big that she could jump over the puddles. And when Sarah jumped the yellow boots with the red stripes went *WHOOSH!*

It was a big sound for a big girl. And Sarah was very happy.